The Willow Flute

A NORTH COUNTRY TALE

The Willow Flute

A NORTH COUNTRY TALE

Written and Illustrated by
D. William Johnson

Little, Brown and Company
BOSTON   TORONTO

FIRST EDITION

T 03/75

Library of Congress Cataloging in Publication Data

Johnson, Dana William.
  The Willow Flute: a north country tale.

  SUMMARY: Lost in a blizzard in the woods, Lewis
Shrew stumbles into an empty house where he finds a
flute that heralds the coming of spring.
  [1. Spring—Fiction] I. Title.
PZ7.J63163No [E]   74-13183
ISBN 0-316-46756-1

Published simultaneously in Canada
by Little, Brown & Company (Canada) Limited

PRINTED IN THE UNITED STATES OF AMERICA

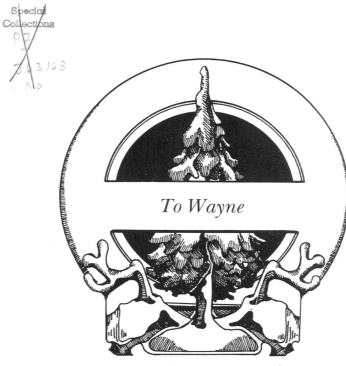

To Wayne

and my family

LEWIS SHREW lived in the middle of a great
forest. It was winter there and the snow was piled
high round the windows.

One March day toward evening, Lewis put on his boots and his old overcoat, his muffler and his mittens to go out into the white woods to gather twigs for his stoves. He would stack all the twigs in a pile as he gathered them and afterward, tie them in a bundle to carry home.

When Lewis stepped outdoors and sniffed the air,
the woods seemed somehow changed. The nearby
pond was encrusted with ice as on the day before,

the willows were covered with frost, and fresh snow had fallen. But the scent of warming branches colored the afternoon, and a hint of springtime swirled in the wind.

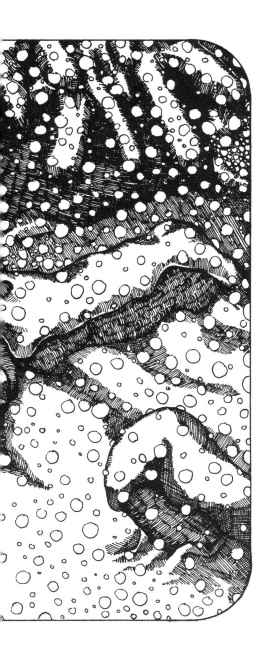

With thoughts of April easing his work, Lewis bundled his twigs, brushed the snow from a log, and then sat down to rest. The wind whispered through the treetops, and it was so quiet that soon he had drifted into a deep slumber. Snow began to fall, and as day dimmed into evening it got deeper and deeper and deeper until it was higher than his head.

14

Night had fallen when Lewis awoke. The sudden storm had run its course, and the moonlit snow pressed in all around him. He was so amazed it was no use trying to recollect where he was. The cold had numbed his paws, and he longed for his house and a cheery fire.

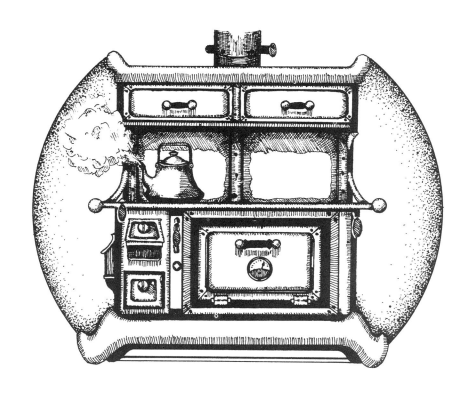

16

Pushing the snow away from himself, he soon made a little room. Mindful of hungry owls overhead, he dared not clear a way to the surface, so every minute found him growing colder than before.

Deciding it was senseless to sit buried there, he set out tunneling. But unable to see a familiar tree or thicket he knew, he went in the wrong direction.

Digging through the cold, heavy snow, he bumped into tree trunks and tangles of willows. Feeling more frightened with each turn, he lost his muffler and tore his mittens on sharp thistles.

Lewis dug through the night to sounds of distant coyotes and snow falling from the evergreens. The insides of his boots were wet, and his paws ached from the cold. Then, as his hopes of reaching home began to flicker, he suddenly struck on something sounding large and hollow.

Clearing the snow away, he found himself in the dimmest light of dawn at a weather-beaten door. A note was on it saying: *The Bird, whistle please.* The message puzzled Lewis, and he wondered who had put it there.

24

Since time had set the door ajar, Lewis, sniffing and glancing around, carefully looked inside.

It was a musty old room with a small window. An iron bedstead was tumbled awry in the corner. A row of dusty jars stood quietly along a rafter, and sooty things lay in shadowy heaps about the floor. A shutter clattered in the wind, yet Lewis sensed nothing to fear.

Creeping in and winding through the shadows, he climbed to a ledge by the window. Shedding his

mittens and boots, he pushed aside the cobwebs and peered out over the snow and the frozen pond.

As Lewis watched the sun rise through blustery clouds, the day seemed a bleak one. The trees stood bent in the wind, and the snow was so deep that his house was hidden, as lost as his muffler.

Turning, Lewis noticed a little willow flute amid the wreckage on the floor. Retrieving it to the windowsill, he began to play quietly to lift his downcast spirits. The flute made a soft whistling sound like certain birds on summer evenings.

32

As Lewis played, the gray sky invited the sun to climb higher, and the wind grew steadily warmer. Icicles slowly dripped from the roof, turning the snow beneath them to slush, and gradually the pond began to thaw.

Snow was soon melting, pulling back from the tree trunks and laying bare whole patches of ground.

Small birds, anxious at the sound of nearing thunder, fluttered in the branches of an old poplar.

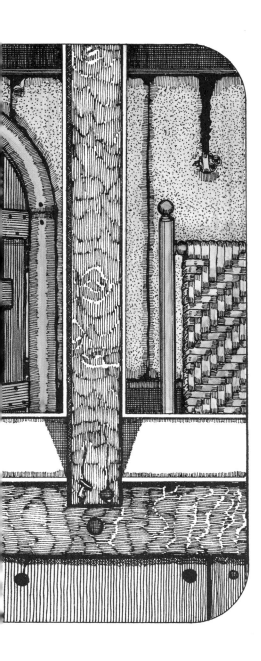

Lewis watched the darkening sky as he played and his song drifted into the forest.

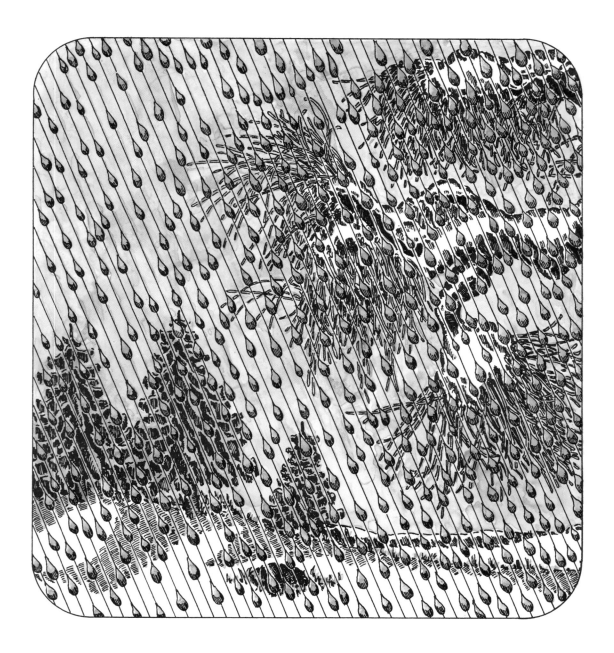

Rain began to fall, pelting the woods and the snowfields, spattering the windowpanes, and running from the roof, gently easing winter's grip. When the rain had passed, the drifts had grown smaller, and Lewis spied his house among the glacier lilies.

Lewis took the flute and scrambled outside, heaving a deep, happy sigh as he felt the muddy forest floor beneath his feet again. Water collected in puddles and trickled across the newly thawed earth.

He paused to breathe the good air. The sun
sparkled through the trees and caught on the won-

derful flute; a robin landed in a pine tree and green
things were thinking of growing.

As the birds sang of spring's return to the North Country, Lewis put the flute to his lips and added his own cheerful song.

He felt the breeze on his face; he smiled at the sun,

and then he went home.

THE END